TIMBERLINE DAVIS

NOV. 2017
Regards—

Timberline Davis
CARROLL CO, GA

The Turnip Coast

For The Young And Old

**SPECIAL FIRST PRINTING
"COLLECTORS EDITION"**

LARGE PRINT

The characters in this book exist only in the mind of the Author. The characters have no relation whatsoever to anyone bearing the same name or names. The characters were not inspired by any individual known or unknown to the author. All incidents and all locations are pure invention

PRINTED IN THE UNITED STATES OF AMERICA

ISBN: 978-0-9835495-6-7

Foreword

The most beautiful people in the world live in a sheltered out-of-the-way stretch of land adjacent to some sea cliffs of Great Britain.

Those beauteous and fair people living in that strip of farmland are farmers that grow and sell turnips.

That cloudy expanse of land called "Turnip Coast" is perpetually overflowing with fragrance and greenness.

The sea breezes are pleasant being continually warmed by an uncharted ocean stream.

Robert and Margaret Montgomery live on a turnip farm with two sons, David and Huegly. The Montgomery farm is almost in the center of Turnip Coast.

Their incredible story is being written only for you and will be dedicated to you, the young at heart.

Father Time is lurking not far behind, always trying to lasso the unwary; so I am putting forth my most energetic and painstaking effort as I take up an inactive pen and delve into the story's past and come forward into the eventful present.

Trying not to be overcome with misgiving, at times my barely discernible thoughts are only echoes in my mind.

From placid to dismay, this incomparable Turnip Coast tale is for the searching and inquiring, written only to delight, entertain and bring joyful happiness to you.

Sincerely,

Timberline Davis

Chapter One

Have we erred in not telling you that those beautiful people of Turnip Coast were also showered with fabulous gifts? Each person possesses a different gift, so unusual, it almost borders upon the supernatural.

My name is David Montgomery. I am Robert and Margaret Montgomery's son.

When I was a teenager, my older brother, Huegly, was a whiz at playing cards. He could win every card game he played if he wanted to.

Next door to us lived my Aunt and Uncle with their teen-age daughter, Avencia Montgomery. She could speak many languages. Probably not every language, but I have never seen or heard a language she could not speak.

My gift is a relationship with numbers. I can divide, subtract, multiply and add numbers as fast as you can write them down.

We don't know where our mystical gifts came from, but they are always there and we know how to use them.

On Saturday evenings, people from farms all around came to our house to visit. The old folks sat around the open fire telling lost stories and tall tales. It was a grand time for the children.

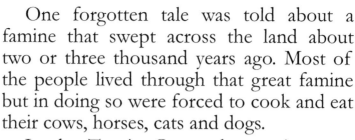

One forgotten tale was told about a famine that swept across the land about two or three thousand years ago. Most of the people lived through that great famine but in doing so were forced to cook and eat their cows, horses, cats and dogs.

In the Turnip Coast, the turnip crops never failed and never faltered. The people survived by learning to eat turnips three times a day.

In the morning everyone ate turnip bread covered over with turnip gravy. They ate baked turnips and fried turnips. For dessert they ate turnip cookies and turnip cake.

The question has been asked many times; was it the soil, the climate, or eating turnips three times a day that down through the centuries was the causation of the people's attractiveness and handsomeness and the receiving of those mysterious fabled gifts.

That question has never been fully answered with complete satisfaction by anyone.

Chapter Two

My teen-age cousin Avencia, living next door, had a fantasy for becoming an actress. She expended a lot of energy playing the showy actress game.

Her mother, always encouraged her to live her dreams. She seemed to enjoy the actress games about as much as Avencia.

In a clothing catalog from the big city, she bought the most expensive and breathtaking actress clothes that can be had.

Her mother wouldn't let her go about town alone, so she chose me to be her escort. Avencia ordered me the most lavish and handsome clothes I had ever seen.

When we went into a town together, wearing our remarkable clothes, we were a sight to behold.

One day, her mother was going to a town outside of Turnip Coast to buy some needed supplies. Avencia and I, dressed in our fine clothes, were going along to revel and star in her secret actress game.

Working in the turnip fields everyday with beautiful people, I don't take notice of their beauty. This day, Avencia with her fantastic make-up and wearing pink lipstick was as dazzling and gorgeous as one can be.

The way Avencia and her mother smiled and approved of me with my new expensive clothes, I thought I must be good-looking also.

In town, Avencia and I walked into the lobby of a large building. With kind smiling faces, we stood tall. We pretended to be celebrities with fame and glory.

In the large lobby all activity stopped and everything became real quiet. Everyone was looking at us. They were wondering, *Who can those fabulous movie stars be?*

Every young man in the big room looked at Avencia and knew within his heart, that at last he found the perfect lady to become his wife.

All the young ladies were looking at me and had fallen in love with me at first glance. It was a grand feeling being in a place where most everyone loves you.

Occasionally, Avencia would speak to me from across the way in beautiful French or Portuguese. I would nod to her and pretend to understand.

Everyone marveled and was amazed at the sensational young couple that had come among them.

The next day, as both of us worked in the turnip rows, with grand feelings, we relived all of that golden experience.

However, we both knew that we would never leave the job that we enjoyed more than anything in the world . . . the growing of turnips.

Chapter Three

In those almost forgotten days of long ago, the finger of evil and some underhanded bad spells were cast upon me.

I was only six years old back then but I knew what the word kidnapped meant.

I was captured and locked in a crazed woman's basement bathroom. After three days and three nights, I finally realized that I was the victim of a real kidnapping. I feared I would never see my loving mother, Margaret, again.

My ordeal of misery and suffering began on a Saturday morning. Mother took my older brother, Huegly and me to a nearby town to buy school supplies. I was starting first grade.

All of the wide-awake, hard working ladies of Turnip Coast are excellent drivers and my mother was no exception.

She was driving Dad's rickety old pickup truck. With full attention, our three sets of keen eyes were watching the roads and bridges ahead. We were not unlike a crafty old hawk with its squinty eyes looking all around searching the nooks and crannies for a tasty meal.

My dad's pickup rode pretty good on our smooth country road. We were always so

excited to leave Turnip Coast and go over to visit an unfamiliar town.

At times, we sat watching the people of those towns scurry back and forth, trying to figure out what they were up to.

Starting to school in the first grade was a brand new experience for me. My excitement and fright were flowing outward about equal. I thought if I could be in the same class-room with Huegly I wouldn't be afraid.

I leaned over to Mother and spoke to her in a low quiet voice trying not to disturb her concentration.

"Mother do I need to start in the first grade? I want to be in the third grade with Huegly. I can already read better than he can, and you know I have a magic understanding of numbers."

"Yes, honey, I know that's true, but I'll have to talk to the teacher about that."

"Mother I'm helping Daddy in his work-shop. When we get to the store could you buy me a pair of pliers?"

She looked at me with questioning eyes. I said, "Please?"

"Son ,why don't you just use his?"

"His are all greasy." I replied, "And they get my hands and clothes dirty."

Here was a child trying to preserve the lost art of keeping clean and that appealed to my mother's insight.

"All right, David, when we get to the store you can get a pair of pliers."

I thought to myself, *My mother, Margaret, is not only beautiful and kind, but she is filled with common sense and wisdom.*

Chapter Four

Little did we know that the new pair of pliers that Mother bought me would save my life. Without those pliers I wouldn't be here telling you any of this today.

In the months that followed, every time Mother went out to the workshop, she would go over to the workbench and look for those pliers. When she found, them she would hold them in her hands and close her eyes with heartfelt thoughts of thankfulness.

Unknown to me, an old woman in the store had been secretly watching me. My being from Turnip Coast, I was the most beautiful child she had ever seen.

She decided then and there that she was going to take me home with her. I was going to be her new son.

With the pair of pliers that I wanted to buy in hand, I was taking them up to the counter when the old woman approached me. "Son will you help me take these bags out to my car?"

"Yes, Ma'am, but I'll have to go ask my mother first."

"This will only take half a minute, there's no need to bother your mother with that."

All of the people living in Turnip Coast are trustworthy so I didn't realize there were mean spirited people out there lying in wait to trick you and hoodwink you.

"Yes, Ma'am, I'll help you."

With an unusual smile that seemed forced to me, she said, "You bring that small bag over there and I'll take this large one." We picked up the bags and took them out to her car.

Her driver opened the rear car door and she placed the bag she was carrying on the back seat and then stepped back. I put the small bag on the back seat next to hers.

I turned to go and that's when her driver grabbed me. He cupped his big hand over my mouth, and with a choke-hold on me, pushed me into the car.

In a hateful, bad tempered voice he said, "You make one sound, you snotty reject, and I'll break your scrawny neck."

I saw right then that being kidnapped was not a very good predicament to be involved in.

The old woman drove her car across town to her house and around to the back door. They caught hold of my arms and took me into the basement and locked me in the basement bathroom.

I looked all around the bathroom and there was no way to escape that I could see. I knew without a doubt this was going to be my new home for the rest of my life.

Chapter Five

On the fifth day, the driver came into the bathroom carrying a razor-sharp butcher knife. He was being real quiet, as this was the old woman's naptime and he didn't want to wake her.

I was sitting on a small cot that had been placed in the bathroom for me to sleep on.

Pointing to the stool, then in a real quiet but gravelly and dreadful voice, he said, "Come sit on the stool." That was a strange request and I wondered, *What does he want me over there for?*

Then it dawned on me, he was going to kill me and he didn't want to mess up the mattress on the bed with blood. It would be a lot easier for him to clean blood off the tile floor than trying to clean a blood soaked mattress.

He put the sharp butcher knife to my throat. Being razor sharp, it was already trying to cut my throat and it hurt.

I was shaking with fright. I knew I had to come up with something quick or I was a goner.

I found out that day, that every second in one's life is precious. I had to stall for time and try to live as many of those precious seconds as I could.

Stalling for time, I asked him in a scared squeaky voice, "Are you going to kill me? Why are you going to kill me? I haven't done anything. Did the woman tell you to do this? She likes me."

I kept stalling. "If you kill me they will catch you and hang you."

He answered that by saying, "Yes you are going to die. But I am not going to kill you. You are going to commit suicide."

"I can't commit suicide, I don't know how."

"Well don't you worry about that, I'll show you how."

He pressed the knife harder, getting ready to rake it across my throat. I could already see myself lying on the floor with my head half cut off.

There came a knock on the door. The old woman called, "Driver, are you in there?"

"Yes, Ma'am, I'm here."

"Would you come upstairs? I dropped a jar of jelly on the floor and I need you to help me clean it up."

"Yes, Ma'am, I'll be right there."

I said, "Wait. Why do you want me to commit suicide? There must be a reason."

"Well," he replied, "I overheard the old dame talking to somebody on the phone. She said she had found her a new son and

she was going to change her will and leave her house and all her money to him. And sonny-boy, I saw right then that something had to be done."

As the driver went out the door, he turned his head and said to me, "I'll be back at midnight for your suicide." He slammed the door shut, locked it, and went upstairs.

Chapter Six

Why was I being kept alone down there in the basement where I may be killed? I knew the old woman was crazy as a bedbug, but then she was smart enough to know that I must be kept under wraps and hidden until the heat was off.

There I was, held a prisoner on death row, so to speak. I knew I had to come up with some kind of plan, and come up with it fast. My time was about to run out, so I had to get moving.

Could I dig my way out? Yes, if I had two months. The floor was tile over concrete. What about digging out the mortar from around one of those blocks? That was a good idea if I could have found something to dig with, which I couldn't.

Then I discovered the pair of pliers in my pocket. I said out loud to myself, "I stole these pliers." But I remembered, they were kidnapped along with me, so they were not really stolen they were kidnapped pliers. That relieved my mind somewhat.

I looked all around trying to figure out how to use a pair of pliers to break out. Then I saw it. My escape plan fell into place. I would pull the hinge pins out of the door hinges, then I could open the door.

I went over and tried to pull the lower hinge pin out but it had been driven in with a hammer and I couldn't pull it out. Right then, I knew I was a gone-gosling.

Shaken and defeated, I went over and sat down on my cot. I leaned over with my head in my hands and had a good cry.

It was getting late. Midnight was not far off. Finally with doggedness and new determination I went back to the door and carefully studied those hinge pins.

I caught hold of the knob on top of the lower pin with the pliers and started twisting it back and forth. In about ten minutes I pulled it out.

Then I started working on the top pin. Same thing, in about ten minutes or so I pulled it out.

I opened the door just enough so I could squeeze through. I went over and looked out the basement window. It was already dark outside.

I tiptoed all the way to the front door, so far so good. I turned the key in the door and it made a loud click. I heard the woman's rocking chair upstairs move.

She came to the top of the stairway and yelled down at me. "What are you doing? How did you get out?" She started screaming for her driver to come and catch me.

He came out of his back room and saw me and started running towards me as fast as a jackrabbit. I knew it was curtains for me this time for sure.

I opened the front door, went through and slammed the door behind me. I still had the key in my hand and I turned around and locked the door an instant before he grabbed hold of the knob and rattled it.

Now he had to go to the back door to get out of the house to catch me.

I'm a good runner and when he got around to the front of the house looking for me, I was long gone.

Chapter Seven

Making my escape through the middle of town I wanted to walk slowly and not arouse any suspicion; but with a wild man, with his fortune at stake chasing after me, I couldn't afford to walk along, as my dad says, with courtliness and respectability.

After running about a city block I looked back and saw him out on the sidewalk coming after me, running at a fast clip. He was not a fast runner but with his long legs he was covering lots of ground.

After running another block on this dimly lighted street, I saw two bully type guys. They were sitting on their front steps waiting for somebody to come along that they could rob. They jumped out on the sidewalk with arms outstretched and grabbed me.

I turned numb all over. I knew my number was up this time for sure. I lunged, twisted around, and broke free, then I was off and running. All they had left of me was half of my shirt.

I kept on running as fast as I could because now there were three wild men chasing after me.

A wild-eyed six year old boy full of fright; running all-out through the middle of town with three persons chasing him is a plain sign of law breaking or a runaway.

I didn't see the two policemen waiting for me in the shadows up ahead. As I ran on toward them, they stepped out of the shadows ready to grab me. They had lots of experience catching runaways so they didn't have any doubt that they would catch me without any trouble.

Just as they grabbed for me, startled, I jumped high in the air spinning around and went racing down a side alley.

They couldn't believe I had escaped them. Not to be outdone they entered the chase.

When the three persons following me saw the police, all three of them stopped chasing me and turned back.

The alley was paved with cobblestones, what my daddy called Belgian-blocks, being ballast removed from the holds of ships. They sure were slippery and risky to run over.

I was used to running over turnip rows when my brother Huegly and I played, so I sailed over those stones easy as pie. Right off one of the policemen turned his ankle and they stopped running.

I came out on the road leading to our farm and I breathed a sigh of relief for I knew then I was home free.

As I went walking down our road at a fast pace, occasionally a police car would go by. I would hide in the bushes on the side of the road so they wouldn't see me. I wondered why so many police cars were going back and forth on our road.

I thought about my mother, surely she must be worried to death about me. She might even be thinking that I am dead and be crying. With those terrible thoughts going round and round in my head, I was filled with worry and sadness.

When I got to our house a police car was in the yard and then I realized they must be out searching for me.

I opened the front door and stood there with my hair all messed up. I'm sure they were startled when they all looked up to see me standing there; my face dirty, only half a shirt on and in a complete state of untidiness.

I smiled with a heart overflowing with joy and said, "Mother, Daddy, I'm home."

Chapter Eight

It was in the early morning twilight when it appeared. There coming towards us was a giant fireball.

I was fifteen years old and my kidnapping nightmare of years ago could be called a forgotten memory.

I was looking out the kitchen window early that morning going about my chores. I saw what appeared to be a white-hot star coming straight toward the window. It was burning its way through the low hanging clouds and leaving behind a glowing white trail.

In less time than the batting of an eye, the house, the yard and the countryside were lit up with a white blinding light. It was even brighter than a limelight or the sun shining down at noontime, yet there was no heat to be felt or noise to be heard.

Dad, walking across the yard doing his chores froze in his tracks. He stood there with outstretched arms and stiffened fingers spread wide apart. He had the appearance of a chalk-white statue; a statue frozen in time.

I quickly looked out another window and saw the fireball travel on for fifty miles before disappearing into the forested hills.

Dad fell to the ground trembling and was severely stricken with a nervous condition from which he never fully recovered.

In my boyish mind filled with book learning from Mother teaching me at home and helping me receive my high school diploma early, I thought that my Herculean dad only had a temporary nervous condition.

Nevertheless, Dad sure suffered with fireball misery. He said a fireball was the harbinger of bad luck and misfortune, although he never figured out what the sign or fore-warning was trying to tell him.

Every night at the supper table, he would say, "well, no bad luck today, or "well, nothing damaging happened today."

He thought about all kinds of mishaps, terrible accidents and catastrophe, but not once did he think about our family. We worked too hard, were all too strong and healthy for any adverse condition to befall us.

About three months later we suffered a horrible tragedy. Afterwards, as the months and years rolled by, the fireball with its signs and warnings was never mentioned in our household again.

Chapter Nine

Daddy's fireball premonition came to pass that dismal day. Darkness and gloominess descended upon our family.

My mother, Margaret Montgomery's number was called. She was destined to die on this day at sundown. Without trumpet flourishes or fanfare, she accomplished that foreboding task.

My mother was the most beautiful lady living in Turnip Coast and probably the most beautiful woman in the whole world, but on that fateful day, her stunning beauty couldn't save her.

My mind begged and questioned, why did she have to die, she was so young and healthy. Well, I was told the schedule of destiny is written and set in stone. It cannot be delayed or postponed.

Mother got out of bed early that morning and was at the woodstove cooking breakfast. She was with child and the baby was due in another month.

Over at the washstand she filled a heavy iron kettle with water to be heated. When she set the kettle on the stovetop a sharp vicious pain struck her in the stomach causing severe flashes of sickness.

With urgency in her voice she called out to me, "David come quick and help me, I think I'm having my baby."

She lay down on the bed crying out in pain. "Mother, I don't know what to do and Daddy is way down in the valley cutting wood."

She looked at me with sad pitiful eyes. "Well, go call Huegly then, I've got to have some help."

In a panic, I ran out on the porch, cupped my hands around my mouth, and started screaming for Huegly.

Huegly came to the house running. "What's the matter?" He asked.

I answered. "Mother is having a baby."

"I don't know what to do, I'll stay here with her, go get Daddy."

I started running across a big field filled with rows of turnips. It was hard going, but finally, I saw Daddy. I was screaming and waving my arms. Daddy heard me and turned around.

I screamed at Daddy. "Come to the house quick, Mother is in labor with her baby."

Daddy, trembling and shivering, ran by me and yelled. "She's not due to have her baby for another month." I took in running after Daddy and it was all I could do to keep up.

Daddy went into the house and I lay down on the porch gasping for breath. While I lay there I could hear Daddy inside saying over and over, "Oh no, oh no."

It's hard to explain, but I could feel a cold draft of air that I took to be the Death Angel hovering above.

Chapter Ten

Dad came out on the porch with a ghastly expression on his face. "David, your mother is dying. Run over to the neighbor's house and tell somebody to go call the Doctor."

At that time the phone line only ran from town out to the country store.

"And David tell one of the ladies to come over here just as quick as she can."

I jumped up and began running toward our neighbor's house as fast as I could. When I got close to their house I saw the two ladies out riding their horses coming straight up the road toward me.

I commenced waving my arms and screaming. "Come quick, come quick, it's my mother."

The ladies pulled the horses up before me and stopped. One of the ladies asked, "What's the matter with your mother?"

"She was lifting something heavy in the kitchen and now she is trying to have her baby a month early. And Daddy said tell you she is losing lots of blood and is getting real weak."

"My goodness." She said. "Marge, you go to the store and call the Doctor, and I'll go on over and see if I can help."

She turned the horse around and rode toward our house with great haste. The other lady rode off towards the store, her horse in a full gallop.

I ran back home as fast as I could which was pretty slow because I was completely worn out by now. When I got home I was all shaky and unstable.

The lady's horse was standing there tied to the porch railing. He watched me as though trying to figure out what I was up to. The horse had never seen anyone go up porch steps and then lay down on the floor.

I must have dozed off. Hearing a noise, I sat up and looked around just as the Doctor and a girl about my age went in the front door and on into the house.

In a couple of minutes the girl came out on the porch and came over to me. "Are you David?"

"Yes ,I am." I replied.

"My name is Margaret the same as your mothers. I spoke to your mother and I said to her, 'Miss Margaret, my name is Margaret also. I am the Doctor's girl.'

"Your mother looked closely at my face and said to me, 'You are the one.' She gave me her gold wedding band all covered with stars. 'This is a magic ring, keep it in a safe place. Someday when it comes time for you to wear it, strange happenings will be revealed to you.' "

"I didn't know what to do so I looked over at Mr. Montgomery and he nodded yes to me and I took the ring."

Margaret and I continued talking for a short while and we were really attracted to one another. "Your mother is so beautiful." Said Margaret.

Huegly came stumbling out onto the porch. He was white as a sheet. With tears streaming down his face, he said to me, "David, Mother's precious little girl-baby is dead and from what I can tell, it looks to me like Mother has lost most of her blood and is about dead too. The Doctor told Daddy if we had a hospital to take her to, they could save her."

I already knew what Huegly was going to tell me, but nevertheless after his mournful words were spoken I was overcome with sadness and grief.

My kind loving mother, Margaret, died that day at sundown. My heart was broken. After our living through that dreadful day, no one in my family was ever the same again.

Chapter Eleven

The Doctor filled out two sets of death papers, one for Mother and one for the girl-baby and then walked out on the front porch.

Little Margaret came over to me and looked into my eyes. "David, I love you." She whispered. "You are the kindest and most beautiful person I have ever seen. I will remember you in my prayers tonight." Then she kissed me tenderly.

That was the sweetest kiss I have ever had. If she wanted to kiss me again sometime that would be fine with me. But the road she is traveling and the road I am traveling are far apart and I know there is no chance that I will ever see her again in my lifetime.

Then the Doctor and his lovely daughter went to their car and drove away.

Inside, in a gentle voice, I said to Daddy, "All her life, Mother wished for a baby girl that she could love, play with, and care for.

"In death, Mother has been deprived of watching her little baby girl grow up, flower and mature. It was not to be.

"Her fairy-tale wishes and her fondest dreams with all her fantasies and desires have been cast into the grave with her."

Huegly said, "That's right Daddy. Mother was surely denied the little girl she always wanted."

Daddy thought about that for a moment. "We need to fix that."

Daddy wrapped the little dead baby-doll in Mothers never-worn silk petticoat and placed the tiny child in Mother's arms.

I believe Mother smiled; all of us saw it, but afterwards, we were not absolutely sure.

That afternoon it started pouring down rain. It was a cold unpleasant rain that flooded our yard.

Mother with her baby was lying on the bed covered with two sheets. The neighbors came and sat with us during three days and three nights of steady rain.

Mother was cold and stiff and I was fidgety and miserable as she lay there patiently waiting for her burial.

While it was raining, Daddy went out to the barn and built a wooden casket for her.

With Mother holding her baby close, Daddy wrapped them in Mother's prized quilt that was sewn with golden thread and we buried them that way.

They were buried in our family cemetery under the limbs of a holly tree covered with red berries. The cemetery has a cast iron fence with a swinging iron gate.

Huegly and I were proud of the country funeral Daddy gave her. He made sure that in death, she could finally have and hold a baby daughter.

Every Sunday, Daddy takes some flowers over and places them on her grave. He talks to Mother and asks her how their little daughter in the silk petticoat is getting along, but Mother never answers or gives any reply.

Mother never wore her silk petticoat, she was always saving it for something grand some day, but that grand some day never came.

Chapter Twelve

The giant fireball presumed to be foretelling Mother's death was a heartrending memory that lingered in our minds and perplexed us to no end. We really enjoyed the precious years we spent with our Margaret.

Happiness looks small when you hold it in your hand but when you let it go, you learn how big and glorious it is.

Touched with sadness, then joy, from time to time we summon up those memories and examine them. Many times all throughout our lives we live them again over and over.

In the days and years that followed Mother's death, Daddy was never the same. Without Mother to cheer him on and help him, he lost all interest in the farm.

He had only one thing on his mind. He wanted to leave this place and travel across the water. Daddy wanted to find and live in that fabulous new turnip farming land in the southern Blue Ridge Mountains.

He had a friend who sold his farm on Turnip Coast and went over there. Every day, Daddy tried to find him. Every farmer he saw he asked them if they knew the address of his lost friend across the water, so that he might contact him.

Also, Mother's death filled my brother, Huegly, with remorse and futility. He took to foolish drinking to deaden his pain and bring comfort to his rack of worries.

I tried my dead level best to talk some sense into his head, but he wouldn't listen. Mother was Huegly's haven and his driving force. No matter what kind of trouble he got into, she never scolded him.

In a short time, Huegly became a changed person. He changed first in heart by the loss of his mother, then he changed in body by drinking rotgut whisky and cheap bootleg whiskey distilled through automobile radiators.

Every day he poisoned his mind and body with lead from those radiators. What I'm trying to tell you is, I was watching Huegly's beautiful healthy body deteriorate. His mind was being consumed and eroding away.

Daddy saw what was going on with Huegly. He was so worried and bewildered that he tried day and night to find a way to relocate him and our family to a new land and a new life.

In this hectic life we are living today, deaths, outside forces, and unwanted entanglements cause the most accomplished and praiseworthy people to fall by the wayside and enter a merciless and calloused life.

That wayward life if not caught and changed in time leads to wickedness and wrongdoing in that person.

Every day, Daddy and I wanted to step forward and restore our sickly Huegly with his addled mind and poisoned body, but nothing we said or did helped him.

We saw that Huegly's mind was gone. We knew we could not change him. It was a lost cause.

Chapter Thirteen

Out in the mailbox there came a letter all faded with age. The yellowed letter had three stamps on it to cover the higher cost of postage that we now had.

Daddy handed the old letter over to me and I was amazed when I saw the beautiful handwriting. The flawless, old-fashioned writing on the blanched envelope was a mystery to me.

Curious and puzzled, I handed the letter back. "Daddy, that's the strangest letter I have ever seen. Open it up and lets see what it says."

We never found out why that letter looked so old. The secret behind that mystery was hidden somewhere over in the southern Blue Ridge Mountains; a land across the water.

The letter:

Dear Mr. Montgomery,

To excel in turnip farming and reap the magic of a rich black soil, all you need to do is find and travel on that golden road leading into the southern Blue Ridge Mountains.

When I moved over here, I found another turnip land, more prolific and possessing more glory and magnificence

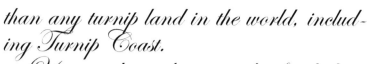

than any turnip land in the world, including Turnip Coast.

You need to relocate to this fertile land that receives almost 100 inches of rain every year.

There is a farm for sale next to mine with a brick and stone house. The grand house is imposing and more like a mansion than not. Best of all, the price on this property has been reduced almost by one half.

Let me hear from you immediately by return mail and I will put money down to hold it for you. I'm getting old and I sure do need a Turnip Coast neighbor that can help me from time to time.

A cabbage farmer has been looking at the place and wants to buy it but the house is too rich for his blood and he can't go.

It's important that I hear from you right away.

I remain your friend and neighbor,

APM.

"Daddy, do you know the old man?"

"Yes, I knew him; he lived down at the crossroads and he was trustworthy and a gentleman as all Turnip Coast people are. I know everything he has written in this letter to be accurate and true.

The next day, Daddy put a letter in the mailbox with a check enclosed addressed to the old gentleman who lived in that land across the water.

On Saturday a real estate salesman from town put a sign out on the road that said "Farm For Sale."

I sure was excited, I figured before long our family would be traveling on a golden road taking us straight into that far-away land, the Blue Ridge Mountains.

What Daddy decided to do, sure appealed to me. It was a big complicated deal, but I was confident that my daddy could manage it.

Chapter Fourteen

Daddy was feverishly working to close his land deal and get Huegly away from this place. Huegly would come home every morning with his pockets full of gambling money.

He couldn't add numbers like me but he could win playing cards. He told me he cheated in every game and I thought sooner or later he would get killed.

Every day I expected the Sheriff to drive up in the front yard with news that he had been shot and killed.

The young men that Huegly gambled with had grown up living miserable lives and were an unfriendly bunch. All of them had pistols in their coat pockets and were fast-handed with a gun.

Huegly now had a deranged mind from drinking lead poisoned whiskey, but it didn't seem to affect his card playing ability.

Daddy had two pistols hidden in the closet, a .45 and a .38. Huegly sneaked out the small .38 and kept it in his pocket all the time. He grew into a brooding, bad-tempered young man. He was not one to be crossed or tangled with.

Huegly and I grew up together. I knew him a lot better than Daddy did; Daddy worked out in the fields all day. He didn't realize what a deplorable and wicked person Huegly had become.

We surely were confronted with a bad situation. I could hardly wait to get on that boat going from Liverpool to Brunswick.

Daddy went into town in his sputtering old pickup and closed the land deal. That grand day we had been looking for finally arrived and happiness and joyfulness came upon Daddy and me.

When Daddy returned home, I asked, "Daddy, where's all the money?"

"I bought a money belt and I am wearing it. I have all the money I own in the belt."

"Well, Daddy, guard it with your life, our future is riding in that belt."

The next day all three of us packed our suitcases with our clothes and all the other belongings we could squeeze in. We left just about everything we owned behind. You can only pack so much in a suitcase.

The next morning the neighbor came to take us to the train station. Huegly was nowhere to be seen.

"What are we going to do?" I asked. "If we don't go and get on the train, we'll miss the boat."

The neighbor told Daddy he would see that Huegly got on the next boat in about a month from now.

Daddy and I picked up our suitcases feeling pretty low. We walked out and locked the

front door behind us. Two of us were now on our way to that land across the water.

Our train-ride to Liverpool and boat voyage to Brunswick was great, but without Huegly we didn't take any pleasure in the experience.

We arrived in the Brunswick seaport about noon.

We went over and bought bus tickets to ride up that golden road to those celebrated turnip fields hidden in a secluded farming area, lost in time, somewhere in the Blue Ridge Mountains.

Chapter Fifteen

We found the old gentleman who wrote us the letter and he helped us with the paperwork buying the farm with the mansion size house.

It took all the money Daddy had and the nest egg that I had saved. Daddy put both our names on the deed. We had enough money left in the bank to pay taxes and live for a while.

"David, David, come quick, a motor has fallen on me and I'm pinned under it.

I was in the house cooking dinner; if I hadn't been standing by the open window I would never have heard him calling, his voice was so weak.

I quit what I was doing and ran out to his workshop to check on him.

We had been living in our new home about six months and Daddy was working on some worn out farm machinery.

I went into the workshop and saw him lying on his back with a big motor on top of his stomach crushing him flat.

I looked at Daddy with tears in my eyes and said to him, "Oh my goodness, Daddy you are hurt real bad."

"Yes, son, I am. See if you can roll this motor off me."

I caught hold of the motor and pulled with all my might, but it was too heavy and I couldn't move it.

Dad passed out and his head rolled over to one side. I yelled real loud, "Daddy hang on, don't you die on me."

I went over in the corner of the shop and got a two-by-four and put it under the motor and rolled it off him.

He opened his eyes and looked at me. "Son, I feel a whole lot better now,"

"Hold on daddy, I'm going to put you in the back of the pickup and take you to the Hospital."

His eyes were closed and he didn't say anything but he was breathing.

I dragged him to the pickup, opened the tailgate and dragged him into the bed of the pickup and closed the tailgate.

"Daddy, don't you try to get up you might fall out."

He smiled at me. "Son, I couldn't get up if I wanted to."

There were only two or three cars on the road and I drove that truck as fast as it would go, about a hundred I guess.

I pulled in at the Hospital emergency room blowing the horn like crazy. About two or three nurses ran out. "My dad is in the bed of the truck hurt real bad. A big motor fell on his stomach and crushed him."

A nurse put two fingers on his throat and said, "His heart is still beating."

Two young men came out with a stretcher. They took him inside and placed him on a bed. I went over to the waiting room and sat down.

In about thirty minutes a Doctor came out and spoke to me. "Your dad's midsection is completely crushed. They have taken him upstairs to see if we can operate on him, but I have bad news for you. He may not last but two or three hours even if we do." When I heard that I thought I was going to die myself.

The Doctor and I went to his room and I sat down beside his bed. In a weak trembling voice I said, "Daddy can you hear me?"

"Yes, Son, I can hear you but I am crushed so bad they can't even operate on me. I know I am not going to make it. I am ready to go, and, Son, everything is left to you.

"It's a real good farm and a real good house. You go find a nice girl like your mother, get married and take care of the place."

"Yes, Daddy, I promise that I will."

He closed his eyes and went into a coma and in about thirty minutes his heart monitor stopped. The nurse shook her head at me and said, "He has passed."

I parked the truck in the yard and went into a quiet empty house. I asked myself, can

this trouble really be happening? Is it all a dream?

Void of thoughts and defying explanation, I called out, "Daddy, are you in here? Daddy, are you in here?"

There was no answer coming out of the emptiness, and I knew then, without a doubt that my endearing dad was eternally gone.

Chapter Sixteen

Farming by myself without my dad was heartbreaking and here's something else, it was backbreaking. After growing and selling several small crops, I saw right off that a one-man operation was at best only a break-even proposition.

Also, to make matters worse, my tractor, truck and farm machinery were all worn out and falling apart.

And there was something else to add to my dilemma, I would never find a wife for a helpmate working all day out in the turnip rows.

What was I to do? I had plenty of money to pay taxes and buy groceries, but very little left for farm equipment.

I supposed I'd have to close down my farming operation for a while and go into town to find a job.

Dad wanted me to marry a girl exactly like my mother but that was impossible, of course.

I read in a magazine about how to find a wife. The article said, don't try to find the perfect woman because she might be looking for the perfect man, whom everyone knows doesn't exist.

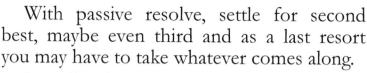

With passive resolve, settle for second best, maybe even third and as a last resort you may have to take whatever comes along.

I really didn't understand that writer's thinking. His article didn't appeal to me very much.

Every time I go into town for supplies, I see a big building about seven stories high I guess and it's spread out all over the place. I was told that it was a gigantic banking, insurance and brokerage firm.

They said that the company paid the highest salary of anybody, and they treated all their employees like part of the family.

And because of that, everybody and his brother, trying to get hired on, went over there. Everybody filled out an application and then your name was placed on a waiting list.

Well, they paid a high salary so I knew that was the place for me.

I decided to go into town Monday morning and fill out an application. I have just turned 19 years old and they might hold my young age against me.

Then I thought, I am a Turnip Coast person and everyone says we are the most beautiful people in the world so my looks may be an advantage and give me a slight edge.

I remembered those days of long ago when Avencia and I went into town pretending to be celebrities. You know if they have girls working in the employment office those movie star tactics might still work today.

I believed getting a job was a good plan. I didn't have any animals so I could lock up the house and out buildings while I was working.

I tossed and turned in the bed Sunday night dreading going into town on Monday morning. *Will everybody laugh at me when I drive up in a pickup truck, all dirty with black smoke pouring out the exhaust pipe?*

I wondered, in the great scheme of things, are other people nervous and filled with fright when they go out looking for that first job?

I would soon dress my best and put in a Turnip Coast appearance inquiring about that first job. Then I'd find out what destiny had in store for me.

Chapter Seventeen

On Monday morning awash with stress, I crawled out of bed having nagging pain gnawing at my spirit. After taking a shower I found Dad's closet to be full of splendid clothes.

Dad was thinking about finding a new wife as he was in desperate need of a helpmate.

I picked out a marvelous outfit with a nice scarf to tuck in. When I got all dressed I looked at myself in the full-length mirror and said, "Amazing."

All my life I had been told how beautiful I was but I never quite believed it, but now I saw it was true.

I drove into town and went over to the company's giant sprawling building and pulled into the wide parking lot. It was filled with late model cars all sparkling in the sunshine.

I parked over on the edge away from everybody where the truck wouldn't be noticed too much.

I walked into the lobby and it was crowded with rich looking people. I thought to myself, *Are all these people here to put money in the bank?*

I stopped in the center of the big room where it was not too crowded. I pulled a pair of white leather gloves out of my coat pocket and with a gentle touch began flapping them over into my left hand.

I looked all around with a Hollywood look appearing to be lost. All the buzz of talking stopped and the lobby became quiet as death. Everyone turned to stare at the famous celebrity.

It appeared that my former Turnip Coast life-style was beginning to pay dividends. Two ladies at the reception desk looked up wide-eyed and I heard one of them say, "I saw him first."

They ran through the crowd and came up to me, "May we help you sir?"

"I am looking for the employment office."

They took hold of my arms. "Sir, we will show you where it is." They guided me down the hall and into the employment office.

The ladies said to me, "This is Julia, the person that does the hiring. I knew at once that this was the lady that I had to bow, flatter and grovel to.

I knew this was my only chance to land a job so I put my hands on the edge of her desk, leaned over and let her look at my face and look into my eyes.

I spoke in a voice, tender, soothing and appealing. "I'm sorry to interrupt the busy schedule of an important lady." I saw her take a deep breath and her heart melt. I believed I had a good chance then.

Chapter Eighteen

I knew what happened in the next two or three minutes would be the difference between keeping my house and farm or losing everything and living in poverty for the rest of my life.

My brother Huegly was probably dead and I had no father and mother. I could not afford to fail.

I was young, knew nothing about the world, and had no one to advise me and guide me. So, not to be an also-ran failure, I had to put forth a true Turnip Coast effort.

My grandmother used to say, "I'm alone in the world and I'm paddling my canoe uphill."

"What is your name?" Julia asked.

"David Montgomery." I answered in a tone so delicate, it played on your ears like a gentle ocean breeze.

"My, that's a beautiful name." She said.

I raised my face up and we looked deeply into each other's eyes and hearts. I knew she had fallen in love with me. But what could I do? I couldn't help it.

"David, sit down here beside me and I will fill out your application for you. Let me see your cards and papers."

I smiled at her and shrugged my shoulders. "I'm from overseas and I don't have any."

"Do you have any references?"

"No I don't."

"Are you a broker or banker" she asked.

"No, I am a farmer and I grow vegetables. The only paper I have with me is the deed to my house and farm."

"Where is your house located?"

"Out Ryan road, the first house on the left."

She thought for a moment. "You don't mean that two million dollar mansion that the lawyer sold, do you?"

"Yes." I answered. "That's the one."

"My goodness, the payments must be large, are you able to pay them?"

"No, I haven't made any payments." I answered.

"Well, don't you know they will foreclose on you?"

"The reason I don't make payments is because the house and farm have been paid for. I own the property. It all belongs to me."

"David, that's amazing. The deed will be all I need. I'll type up all your papers and cards and you can sign everything when you start to work. I have several openings for bankers but the only other job opening I have is in the supply room."

"That will be fine. Can I start to work tomorrow morning?"

"Yes, come to this office first to sign your papers."

She smiled at me and then stood up looking at me with all seriousness. She came over and wrapped her arms around me and gave a long loving kiss.

Everyone in the room clapped their hands. She smiled at them and said, "My long lost brother."

Chapter Nineteen

I walked out to the mailbox and there was a postcard from my brother, Huegly, from Turnip Coast.

I had been working in the supply room about six months and was off that day, it being Saturday. Here was Huegly alive at 24 years of age. I was filled with joy. I didn't believe he knew that his daddy was dead.

I didn't find out the following until later, but at that very moment, my brother, more insane than not, was walking up the gangplank preparing to board an ocean going vessel.

With ticket in hand, he was carrying a heavy suitcase packed full of gambling winnings and one change of clothes.

According to the postcard, his card-playing buddies were trying to kill him and to escape death he had decided to come to the Blue Ridge Mountains in America.

His ticket was taken up and he boarded a small tramp vessel, leaving Liverpool on a voyage bound for the seaport of Brunswick.

By now Huegly had a completely deranged mind brought about by his craving and drinking of tainted rotgut whiskey.

I felt pangs of sorrow for him because all of his sickness of mind and body started at the time of Mother's death.

I am sad to tell you that in the back of his disheveled mind he had hatched up a heinous scheme for cold blooded murder.

When he arrived at his destination, (my farm), and the time was ripe, he would bring his death-dealing plot to the forefront and put it into play.

I think his secret plan was to kill me and then my house and farm would go to him.

Was it Daddy's fault that he didn't take Huegly in hand and forbid his carousing around and wantonness?

Was it my fault that I didn't go with him and protect him when his mind was lead poisoned? But Daddy and I were suffering from Mother's death in our own way, the same as Huegly.

All that thinking was water under the bridge and couldn't be brought back. My mind and body would always be filled with agony and I knew I would continue to suffer to my death from all of this.

Before Mother's death, Huegly was probably the most beautiful, flawless and healthy person in Turnip Coast. But as you can see being a good-looking and grandiose person does not guarantee honesty, truthfulness and uprightness within a person.

At times the most beautiful and loving persons stumble and falter from happenings brought on by unseen or abnormal circumstances.

Chapter Twenty

At my front door, standing there with blood-shot eyes sunken into his pale face, was Huegly, my brother. Several weeks after receiving his unexpected post card, his bizarre arrival had come to pass.

I had been actually dreading this day to no end and it was happening right before me.

I had just come home from work in the late afternoon when he arrived. He arrived in a taxi with a heavy suitcase that he could barely lift.

As the taxi went out the driveway back to town, I was standing there filled with wonder and with more questions than answers.

He began shifting from one foot to the other, struggling with a frustrated attempt at speech that filled my heart with pity and sorrow. With an addled mind he became blustery and disturbing at his failed attempt.

After seeing his decrepit condition and listening to him sputtering, my thoughts were, *The once beautiful Turnip Coast creature standing before me is still my brother, but he has now regressed into the disabled role of non-person.*

I could see wickedness and viciousness in his face.

I tried to enter into conversation with him. "Huegly, Daddy is dead."

Without a blink or a tear he answered. "David, the only thing for sure today is nothing is for sure." That's all that was ever said between us about our father's death.

Many questions began to emerge in my mind. *Did he travel all the way from Turnip Coast in the British Isles to live forever with me? How does he communicate with strangers? How did he manage to travel with a heavy suitcase that great distance alone?*

I picked up his heavy suitcase. "Huegly, come with me and I'll show you a room where you can live." His suitcase was as heavy as though it was filled with magazines.

He went into the middle of the room, pulled off his shoes, then lay down across the bed in his clothes and slept that way all night.

In the morning he came into the kitchen where I was cooking breakfast and asked me did I have any spirits.

My grandma always said that the best treatment for drunkenness was never let them get hold of anything to drink forever more. Folks, that's a tough row to hoe, but it cures you.

I knew he was far-gone, but since he was one of God's children and my brother, I had to get him well if I could. To treat his illness, grandma's remedy was all I had.

I said to him in a kind but firm voice, "Huegly, as long as you stay here, there will be no drinking and I expect you to abide by that rule."

Without drink he got more stable but I saw hatred on his face every day. I never turned my back on him and I always kept my windows and door locked in my room. I worked like a dog at the bank and needed my rest at night.

I hope Mother was not looking down from Heaven watching this spectacle being played out before me.

Little did I know, that Huegly pretending friendly innocence, was now ready to make his move for murder.

Chapter Twenty-One

That fateful day Huegly had been waiting for arrived. While I was at the bank working, Huegly opened his suitcase and brought out the hidden apparatus needed to carry out his hellish murder plot.

Old Saying:

"Plans Made by Mice and Men,

Are Sometimes Reversed in the End."

Huegly was alone at Dad's tractor when his instrument of murder hit critical and a deadly muffled explosion occurred. Components of the tractor were scattered over the field.

After being severed from his body by a metal plate, Huegly's head went rolling and bouncing across the new mown grass.

The death-dealing blast erased his hair and face and a resulting grease smear went sailing through the air. Then his bare skull lay over in the grass looking upwards toward Heaven.

His body was unceremoniously cast into a rosebush's prickly briars. Looking overhead you could see shreds of his clothing hanging on the tree limbs.

At breakfast that morning, I told Huegly that when I got home from work I was going out with the tractor and mow some weeds. Huegly knew that it was time for him to act.

Raising a cover on the tractor, he taped a stick of dynamite on top of the tractor motor. The heat of the motor would cause the stick of dynamite to explode.

After work, I was on the tractor mowing. Huegly was rocking in my favorite rocking chair, already considering it belonged to him.

He sat there watching and waiting for my death. He expected it to come to pass any minute. However, there was one important detail in his sinister plan that he overlooked.

The cooling fan on the front of the motor was keeping the dynamite and motor cool. Huegly was puzzled, he couldn't understand why the dynamite didn't blow.

After mowing about an hour, I stopped mowing and yelled over to Huegly. "I'm going over to the country store before they close to get some things." I got in the pickup and drove away.

Now that the tractor motor was stopped and the cooling fan was not blowing air, the dynamite was beginning to cook.

Huegly went out to the tractor to investigate. He leaned over and touched the stick of dynamite to see if it had come loose.

That's when the history-changing explosion happened, and in this world, Huegly was no more.

Chapter Twenty-Two

When I returned from the store I was appalled as I viewed the ghastly scene bestrewed before me. Crestfallen and dispirited, I went in the house and called the Sheriff.

In about ten minutes, the Sheriff, an ambulance, and a fire-truck arrived in the front yard. The firemen rushed over with an extinguisher. They doused and smothered out the burning tires.

I didn't watch, but the medics put the remains of Huegly in a body bag and carried him to the ambulance and drove away.

The Sheriff said, "He must have filled the water tank with gas and cranked the tractor. A leaky hose caused drops of gas to fall on the hot engine and the vapor caused the explosion."

I figured there might be more to it than that, but I didn't know so I didn't say anything.

I sure was saddened at the outcome of all this. I saw that Huegly's mind was in an addled condition from which I believed he could never recover.

Without having a lot of time to ponder and think all this through, I didn't know exactly what to make of it. I suppose he just wanted me out of the way so he could sell the house and farm and collect a pile of money.

The only good memories I have left in my mind are the happy times in our childhood; joyful days we spent together, growing up in Turnip Coast.

His vile scandalous days of drunkenness and his gambling cheating days would be blotted out and scrubbed from my memory.

Down through the years as I grew older, I still experienced periods of vexation, anguish and despair.

It's almost unbelievable that one of the most beautiful and trustworthy persons from Turnip Coast could not recover from the loss of a loved one.

But you and I both know, all people in this uncertain world, are cast from a different mold.

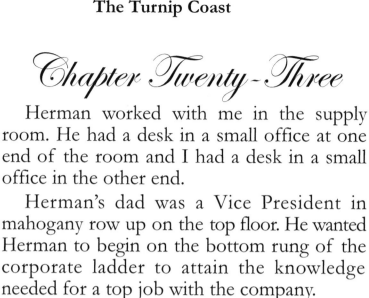

Chapter Twenty-Three

Herman worked with me in the supply room. He had a desk in a small office at one end of the room and I had a desk in a small office in the other end.

Herman's dad was a Vice President in mahogany row up on the top floor. He wanted Herman to begin on the bottom rung of the corporate ladder to attain the knowledge needed for a top job with the company.

I felt sorry for Herman. He thought he was an in-vogue ladies man, but the girls only talked to him because his dad was a VP. He was full of boastfulness and bluster, and had few friends.

The way Herman lived was just a cover for his insecurity, shyness and loneliness. At all times I treated him with respect, dignity and courtesy and we had become the best of friends.

But remember Herman grew up in a different kind of home than I did. My life was spent growing up in Turnip Coast growing and eating turnips. I know that may not sound like much to you, but I have developed a healthy body, beautiful face and notable hidden talents.

At times it is difficult for me, a Turnip Coast person, to live quietly and live an ordinary life.

Herman came in that morning with a big smile and all bright eyed. "Boy, did you see that new receptionist? She's been here a week but today is the first time I saw her. When I go on break I'm going up there and ask her for a date."

I just laughed at him showing my disbelief.

With the haughtiness and conceit that he showed to everyone, he said, "So you don't think I can do it, do you? A ten spot says I can."

His billfold was packed full of money and I only had one bill in mine, barely enough to cover my lunch. I sure hated to go without lunch, but I thought it over and said to him, "I'll bet you ten that you can't and bet you ten that I can."

"Okay you're on, shake on it." He said.

We shook hands on it and went up into the lobby on our coffee break. I sat way off to the side watching and he walked up to her desk.

I couldn't hear what they were saying but pretty soon I saw her shake her head and walk off in a huff.

He came back to where I was sitting, dragging his feet. "David, I owe you a ten spot, I had bad luck. There she is coming back, go try your luck for another ten spot."

I had already combed my hair to perfection and fixed my collar to highlight my Turnip Coast appeal. "Okay, Herman, sit here and watch, I'm on my way."

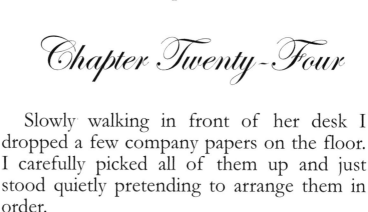

Chapter Twenty-Four

Slowly walking in front of her desk I dropped a few company papers on the floor. I carefully picked all of them up and just stood quietly pretending to arrange them in order.

She looked at my face, studying it carefully. My plan was working. I stood there in silence allowing the import of my beautiful face and incomparable Turnip Coast personage to parade before her.

Overcome with inquisitiveness and awakening, she spoke to me. "Oh, I'm sorry. Do you need some help?"

I just smiled at her and didn't say anything.

She walked around the desk and stood in front of me. With caring and accommodating friendliness, she then spoke to me with a voice of love. "You sure do look familiar."

I just smiled again and looked deeply into her eyes. She touched my face. With a questioning tone she asked, "By any chance are you that little boy I once knew in a land called Turnip Coast?"

I was completely taken by surprise and I asked, "Are you that little Margaret that came to see my sick mother, and as you left, kissed me goodbye?"

She gave out a happy cry. "You're David."

"Yes Margaret, I am David. I can't believe we have found each other."

She put her arms around me and kissed me fervently and affectionately. "David, I have loved you all these years."

"And Margaret, I have loved you since that day long ago when you kissed me goodbye.

For the rest of the day, Herman couldn't believe what he had just witnessed. "What did you say to her?"

"I didn't say very much, I let her do all the talking."

"That's strange, she would hardly talk to me." Said Herman.

Poor puzzled Herman was searching for an answer that would explain to him the loss of two ten spots.

Chapter Twenty-Five

"David why do girls smile at you all the time and never smile at me?"

Herman sat down beside my desk. "And why does everybody like you and all of them hate me?"

I looked at Herman and quickly thought everything through. My brother Huegly wouldn't listen to a word I said but his mind was impaired with lead poisoning, whereas, here was Herman with a brilliant mind.

"It took a long time for you to alienate everyone." I said to him. "And it will take a long time for you to win all of them back. By the way, what did you say to that bank teller this morning?"

Herman looked at me with a perplexed look in his eyes. "I was way off base when I spoke to him. I asked him was he having a turkey for thanksgiving, and he said, 'No not this year.'

"Well if you need some meat," I said, "Let me know and I'll watch for a road-kill for you."

I looked at him and shook my head. "You know that wasn't too nice.

"Now, Herman, I want to tell you some-thing about the teller. His father died back in the summer and they have several huge medical bills to pay. All the family is hard pressed for cash."

"Gosh, if I had known that I would have kept my mouth shut." Said Herman. "What can I do to make amends?"

"Go down to that meat market on the corner and buy a turkey for him and apologize."

Later Herman came back to my office. "David, I did what you said; I bought a turkey for him and apologized. He was so overcome that he came out and cried on my shoulder.

"I was so filled with shame and so touched that I went up to my dad's office and got him to raise his salary to top pay. I gave the teller a signed memo from Dad—CFO, Chief Financial Officer—showing his new higher salary."

He looked at me with the happiest strangest look you ever saw. "Don't you cry again." I said to him.

He laughed with a pitiful little laugh. "No sir, I won't."

Herman left my office and over his shoulder said to me, "David, you are on the bottom rung of the ladder, but you are the smartest person in this company."

Chapter Twenty-Six

Entering the spacious lobby at 4:00 o'clock, I was adoring the beautifying ornamentation at the reception desk. No it was not the colorful vase of flowers I beheld, it was the most beautiful lady in the world, my adorable Margaret.

I eventually found the exact lady my dad wanted me to marry; a lady as kind and as beautiful as my mother.

Together we walked slowly into the company coffee shop. Margaret was walking alongside me with gracefulness and poise.

The impressive couple from Turnip Coast forced all heads to turn and all eyes to stare. As we sat sipping our coffee, I asked Margaret how she got from Turnip Coast to the Blue Ridge Mountains.

Margaret's intricate story began to unfold before me. "Well, David, when my daddy the Doctor came to deliver your mother's baby, I came along with him because your mother's name was also Margaret, the same as mine.

"Daddy had a bad heart but he worked hard all the time. He had a heart attack and there was no hospital to go to. He died that same year.

"My mother died when I was born, so there I was, just six years old and all alone in the world. My aunt and uncle let me live with them. All of these years I have been going to school and helping them raise turnips on their farm.

"They heard about a farm available over here so they sold out everything and came to the Blue Ridge Mountains in America. With no place to go to live, I came along with them.

"Now that I am about grown, they wanted me to have friends and date someone. I came into town, got this job, and live in a motel. The motel costs a fortune, but I haven't found any place to rent that I like."

"Margaret, do you enjoy working for a big company like this?"

"No, David, once the freedom of living and working on a farm gets in your blood, you are never satisfied with anything else. On a farm you work hard at times, but when you get caught up there's plenty of time off to read and sew."

"Margaret, I have a farm with a house that has five bedrooms. You can come and live in my house and you can have any bedroom you want."

"I can't do that, if the company found out we lived in the same house they would fire both of us."

"Yes, you're sure right about that. Haven't you loved me for a long time?"

"Yes, David, practically forever."

"Well, Margaret, at lunchtime tomorrow let's go over to the court house and get a marriage license. On Saturday morning, we can go to the church and the Preacher can marry us."

"My long lost darling David, I know we love each other, I think getting married on Saturday is a good plan."

Chapter Twenty-Seven

On Saturday morning Margaret and I were married. Something almost unbelievable, she was wearing the gold wedding ring circled with stars that Mother gave her many long years ago.

How did Mother know that I was going to marry little Margaret someday? There are still a few scientific oddities in this old world that are not fully understood.

After the wedding ceremony, attended by about five people, we went by the motel and picked up her clothes.

She drove her car behind my pickup truck out to the house that was to become her new home. Margaret got out and looked all around enjoying the picture postcard setting of a mansion with green shrubbery and colorful flowers.

She was so excited and happy that she came over and kissed me. "Margaret, this is where I live and this is going to be our home forevermore.

"And you won't have to work at the office another day if you don't want to. I make enough money for taxes and expenses with some left over."

"Oh, David, there's nothing I would like better than staying home, raising turnips, and

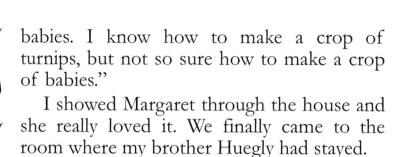

babies. I know how to make a crop of turnips, but not so sure how to make a crop of babies."

I showed Margaret through the house and she really loved it. We finally came to the room where my brother Huegly had stayed.

"These closets sure are enormous." She said, is that your brother's suitcase in the back?"

I had forgotten all about his suitcase. "Yes it is, it's full of books I think, he read all the time."

I slid the heavy suitcase out into the room and opened the lid. It was stacked full of gambling money from bottom to top. I didn't think there was any money in the suitcase because I gave him money to spend most every day.

He had removed the few clothes he had and only the money remained.

With my magic relationship with numbers, in half a minute I knew exactly how much money the suitcase contained.

"Margaret, there's more money here than you would ever believe. I want you to go in to work Monday and turn in a resignation notice. You have been assigned the mission of raising turnips and babies."

Chapter Twenty-Eight

Winter was upon us and Margaret was expecting a baby in the early spring. I went in to work every day and Margaret stayed home.

Herman, who worked with me in the supply room, called Sunday night. He had the flu and was taking sick leave.

On Monday morning I went into work early. The supply room phone rang and a Vice President in the boardroom was out of 24B1 forms and needed some at once.

Immediately I took the forms up there and knocked on the heavy oaken door. The remote control lock clicked and a voice called out. "Come in."

I opened the door and went in. "Here are the forms you ordered, Sir."

On a big board on the front wall were all kinds of charts with zigzag lines drawn on them, running up and down. I was looking at the lines and numbers.

The VP said to me, "The charts look pretty complicated to you, don't they?"

"No Sir, after looking them all over they look real simple to me."

"Well, son, we have the most educated men on the east coast hired to study those charts and make decisions about the market's

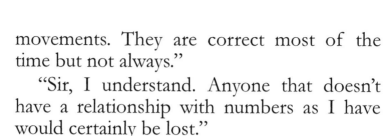

movements. They are correct most of the time but not always."

"Sir, I understand. Anyone that doesn't have a relationship with numbers as I have would certainly be lost."

"What's this relationship with numbers you are talking about?"

"Well, Sir, I can add a row of numbers from the top of the page to the bottom and give you the answer instantly. I can also do the same dividing, multiplying and subtracting.

"My dad could even look at a horse and tell how many teeth he had in his mouth. I'm sure I can do the same thing, but I've never needed to know that ,so I've never tried it."

An older gentleman wearing a dark pin-stripped suit came over. "Joe, what is that I hear about horses teeth?"

"Oh, BJ, this young man has an affinity with numbers and he can tell you exactly which way the line on a chart will move."

BJ came over. "Son, do you know who I am?"

"Sir, I'm not personally acquainted with you, but I've seen you many times. I know that you are Mr. BJ Goodbody, the President of this company."

"Well, son, go up there and study that chart on the left and write down which way you think the line will move."

"I'll study it if you want me to, but I glanced at it when I came in and I already know that by closing time today it will go up over a hundred points." At that time everyone close by laughed at me.

"There's no way in the world it can do that. Said BJ. "It's in an assertive down trend. They have already figured it out over there and they are predicting down 40."

"Oh please, Sir, don't let them send that out, you will lose money. I went up to the chart and wrote, 'up 118 points,' on the side of the chart and everyone smiled.

I said nothing more, then I turned and went out the door on my way.

Chapter Twenty-Nine

I locked up the supply room door at 4:00 o'clock and Mr. Goodbody walked up. "Son are you through down here?"

"Yes Sir, I am."

"Come with me then, I want to show you something upstairs."

We took the elevator and went upstairs and into the boardroom. With a quizzical look he asked, "Son, what is your name?"

"David Montgomery."

"David, look at that chart and see what it did."

"Sir, you know I don't need to look at it, I already know it went up about 118 points."

"David, you made the luckiest guess of anyone I have ever seen, it went up 120 points. Tomorrow morning, come up here before you open the supply room and we will test your guessing ability again."

The next morning, Margaret and I were eating breakfast. We had turnip pancakes smothered in butter and honey. For coffee, we used boiled turnip juice with creamer. Margaret and all the Turnip Coast girls are excellent turnip cooks, possessing hundreds of turnip recipes.

"Margaret, yesterday I was called upstairs to a room where all the market movements are figured out. I gave Mr. Goodbody a number to use on a chart, and of course, the number I gave him was correct. He wants me to come back today and give them today's number.

"Last night after thinking everything through, I decided I'm not going to do that anymore. As soon as they find out I can give them the correct number every day that's all I would be doing. It would soon get out of hand.

"Before long, everybody in the Stock Exchange would be watching me. I know our lives would be ruined. I've definitely made up my mind to never give out another plus or minus number that shows market direction."

When I got to work that morning, Mr. Goodbody was waiting for me inside the door. "Good morning, David, we are running a little late and we need to hurry upstairs."

"Mr. Goodbody, I won't be able to make a number prediction for you anymore."

"Well, I have already told them upstairs that you will give us another number this morning. It will be hard to back down now.

"David, I want you to know that I really like you and I am sorry that it had to come to this. You are a rare individual and I know you have the gift of numbers but I will tell everyone you just made a lucky guess."

As I went to the supply room, the big boss had a face full of frowns and I knew for

a fact that I was in hot water. My job with this company was probably on shaky ground.

My future working with a large company anywhere could be closed down forever, if not forever, then until the cows come home.

Chapter Thirty

As I drove home, all at once it hit me. Speaking the language of business, today I have been fired from my first organizational employment.

Did I feel better or worse for it? I didn't know. Did it change the world? Not much, my truck was the same. It was still skipping and sputtering.

Halfway home, my truck gave out a whistle, a cough, and a death rattle. I believed it was trying to tell me something.

There was an automobile dealership up ahead on the right. I hoped the truck could hold on long enough to get there. I pulled into their parking lot just as the truck made ready to throw in the towel.

When I turned off the ignition key the motor blew up, throwing out a big cloud of smoke. The truck backfired, sounding as loud as a gunshot.

Everybody looked up and ducked, getting ready to run for cover. When they saw the smoke boiling up from my truck, chagrined, they turned and went on about their business.

I took two bricks out of the truck bed and blocked the front wheels. I didn't want the truck to roll into that Lincoln parked in front of me. I was already hobbled with all the millstones I could carry.

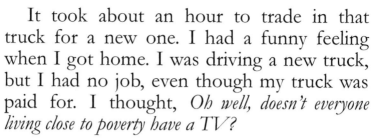

It took about an hour to trade in that truck for a new one. I had a funny feeling when I got home. I was driving a new truck, but I had no job, even though my truck was paid for. I thought, *Oh well, doesn't everyone living close to poverty have a TV?*

When Margaret saw me coming up on the porch, she ran out to me. "Oh David, I am so glad that's you. I was scared to death, trying to figure out who that was driving up to the garage in the middle of the day in a new truck. And David, why are you home in the middle of the day?"

"Well, Margaret, today is the day of days for me. I just got fired from my job and the motor in my old truck blew up. Like it or no, today I am a turnip farmer again. I sure have mixed emotions and I probably shouldn't say this, but I am homesick for Turnip Coast."

"Honey, I have something to tell you that I was never going to say anything about. When we got married and I slipped the magic star wedding ring on my finger, a colorful picture materialized before my eyes and filled my mind with wonder.

"I believe the star ring was trying to show me a future happening. A picture floated before me of a Turnip Coast farm with low hanging clouds overhead. I saw a Colonial Mansion nestled under the trees that had four big columns on the front. I don't know what to make of all this. Tonight we should start talking about it."

Chapter Thirty-One

As the days and weeks passed by, the time came for Margaret to go to the hospital and have her baby.

I was in the waiting room and the nurse came in. "Mr. Montgomery your wife just gave birth to the prettiest little baby boy I have ever seen."

What happened in the hospital was something unheard of and never seen before. Doctors, nurses and workers from all over came to see that beautiful baby. I thought, *This is truly a Turnip Coast baby.*

"Mr. Montgomery, please come with me. The little guy is hungry and crying, we'll take him into Mrs. Montgomery's room and let her feed him with breast milk."

We named the baby boy, Robert, after my dad. Now we had a joyous addition to our family that might erase homesickness from our minds.

Later a mature couple from town came to see the new baby and to get acquainted. They had bought the farm next to us. They were not turnip farmers, not farmers of any kind, really.

They were going to build a castle in the middle of their farm and have a winery. They

would produce and sell grape wine and turnip wine.

Margaret said to me later, "When they get the winery completed, maybe we can sell them our house and farm.

"Every day I get more homesick for Turnip Coast than ever. All the girls that I grew up with and went to school with are now married and live on farms. They are having a grand time. I have a wonderful home but I don't have any friends."

I was as homesick as she, but it was an enormous undertaking to sell everything and relocate to another land.

I received a letter from our neighbor. He made us a standing offer for our land, house, and belongings.

It was a fair offer. Margaret and I were considering it seriously. We thought we would probably sell everything to him.

Chapter Thirty-Two

During Margaret's short stay at the hospital to bear her second child, the homesickness for Turnip Coast was not as pronounced as before.

I knew she secretly wanted a girl but even though she had another boy, her heart was gladdened with cheerfulness and her face was overspread with pleasure.

The builders were working on the big winery castle next door and in two and a half years it was finished. It was a glorious spectacle to been seen from near and far.

Margaret's third trip to the hospital was the fulfillment of her dreams. She brought home twin girls. We sure were having fabulous luck growing a crop of boy and girl babies.

On a rainy morning in the fall of the year, I was in the house playing with the little tykes. I received an important telephone call from a big bank in Charlotte.

The secretary on the line was trying to locate a David Montgomery. "Are you the same David Montgomery that came over to the Blue Ridge Mountains from Turnip Coast in Great Britain?"

I answered, "Yes, that's me. I am that David Montgomery."

"One moment please, the Manager wants to talk to you."

The manager came on the line. "Mr. Montgomery, a lady living in a small town on the edge of a region called Turnip Coast has died. She has no dependents or relatives and she left a will bequeathing all her property to you.

"Our bank here in Charlotte is directing the disposal of her property. We are sending you some legal documents to be signed.

"When you receive the papers, fill them out. Sign them with a notary witnessing the signature and return all of them promptly to us.

"There is money involved here, so send us a blank check and mark it void. We will transfer the money to your bank account."

By the time he finished giving me all those instructions about a fortune coming to me, I was beginning to get a bit nervous.

Margaret came over to me. "Honey, what was that all about?"

"That woman that lost her little boy long ago and kidnapped me to be her new little boy died and has left everything to me.

"Margaret, if this turns out the way I think it will, we can sell everything. Our family can finally go on an ocean voyage to that great land across the water, "The Turnip Coast."

Chapter Thirty-Three

Be it known that everything worked out fine for our family. The selling of our farm and house with all the business transactions were accomplished without any burdensome difficulty.

Everything we had sold: the truck, tractor, the car, farm implements, even the house furnishings, all brought in good money.

Before a friend arrived to take us to the railroad station, Margaret served the family some flavorsome turnip porridge. She made it from that secret recipe that was handed down from her grandmother. You should have seen the four children put away that porridge. They really loved it.

So there we were, our family of six with three suitcases, all on a train traveling south from the Blue Ridge Mountains to the Brunswick Sea Port. The next leg of our journey would be an ocean voyage across the Atlantic to Liverpool.

At a quayside store in Brunswick, Margaret bought the children nylon halters to wear on the ship. The halters had a strong leather snap-on leash with a handhold on the end. Margaret and I didn't want to lose a child overboard on the ship. On deck Margaret always kept them leashed.

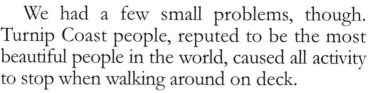

We had a few small problems, though. Turnip Coast people, reputed to be the most beautiful people in the world, caused all activity to stop when walking around on deck.

People stared at us in disbelief. Everyone wanted to be a friend and be seen and photographed with the famous celebrities on board.

When Margaret turned to talk to me, even I couldn't believe how beautiful she was. I suppose I was handsome too, because all the girls wanted to stop and befriend me and get a conversation started with me.

On an afternoon when we finally arrived at the train depot in the middle of Turnip Coast, our family was just about worn out. But tired or not, Margaret and I were overcome with happiness and thankfulness.

The different feel of the Turnip Coast air, the different smell, gave us a sense of warmth and gratification.

My tired family with three suitcases took a taxi ride over to the house on 28 Pavillion Street that a strange woman left to me.

That house on Pavillion Street was predestined to temporarily be our new home for a time.

Chapter Thirty-Four

The house we just moved into was in a small town out on the edge of Turnip Coast. It was a marvelous place and had smart looking furniture.

From the day we moved into that house, Margaret seemed restless. Her mind seemed to be in a state of disorder.

The next day was our wedding anniversary and I was going to the mall to get her a nice present.

Out of the blue it dawned on me what had happened. When we moved back to Turnip Coast, the magic in her wedding ring awakened and was cluttering up her mind.

For an anniversary present, I would get her a wedding ring of her own and store mother's ring away someplace.

The next day at lunchtime, I gave her a present all wrapped and covered with ribbons. All the children crowded around her and wanted to help with the unwrapping.

What they found inside the box was a silk petticoat for her to wear later, on a grand occasion.

Margaret and the children loved that petticoat. I didn't say anything about my mother's silk petticoat of long ago. Someday I will tell them that story.

"Now, Margaret, hold out your left hand."

She held out her hand and I slipped mother's wedding ring off her finger and put a small box in her hand. She opened the box and took out a gold wedding ring covered with a beautiful design. Margaret really liked it and the children thought it was wonderful.

That afternoon, when Margaret and I were alone, she said to me, "David I'm glad you took that magic ring away, since we moved into this house it has been sending me strange pictures and really confusing me.

"Now my mind is clear again and I am a changed person."

"Margaret, the ring is now hidden away in a safe place, but you are obligated to pass it on to a new keeper someday. Before I hid it, I put it on my little finger to see if it would work it's magic on me.

"A colorful picture of a church came floating before me. It showed me walking up the steps and into the church. The church was full of people and they were all watching me.

"There was a casket in the front of the church and the lid was open. I walked up to the casket and looked in to see who was going to die.

"What I saw was an empty casket. Then the ring's floating picture said to my mind, 'No one is going to die.'"

Chapter Thirty-Five

Knowing we were destined to live as the magic ring prophesied was a grand feeling. Knowing we were going to live and farm again in the land of Turnip Coast was also a grand feeling.

But bad news; no farm was available right then, so what must we do?

For three months I have driven over the roads with nothing to show for it. The only land I found was two farms, side by side, with incredible level land, being sold as one parcel, with an incredible high price.

Margaret and I talked about our problems one night and she suggested we go meet with the owners of the land and try to negotiate a lower price.

A woman's insight and intuition hardly ever fails, so I felt that was what we should do.

I called them on the phone and made an appointment to meet with them the next day, Saturday morning.

We decided to give the owners of that land, a family of townspeople, an introduction to beautiful and friendly Turnip Coast personages.

On Saturday morning our family of six, all dressed in shimmering clothes went over to fulfill our appointment.

Our four children with impeccable manners, and Margaret and I with a majestic appearance, went to their front door.

They opened the front door, and, overcome with awe and amazement, invited us in. Bringing out their expensive china dishes, they served us tea and cookies.

After talking farming and land values for a while, the older gentleman said in a conciliatory and accommodating voice, "We have been trying to sell this land for over two years with no success and now after looking upon your family we believe it has been reserved for you.

"We want you to have this land and we will sell it to you for half price. We will still make a fair profit selling it at half price."

The gentleman wrote out a bill of sale and said. Please give us one dollar for a down payment to hold the land."

When we returned home Margaret said to me, "David, a Higher Power is watching over our family and is defending and protecting us."

Chapter Thirty-Six

"Daddy, can we go with you to the four rocks?" Every time I went over to the farm land, the children crowded around me and asked, "Can we go to the four rocks?"

Going to the four rocks for them meant getting out of the house, a picnic on the farm and running and playing among the wild flowers with glorious freedom.

After we paid for the land and received the deed, Margaret wanted to go out to the farm and find the place where the house she saw in her vision was located.

We went out to our new land. I drove up and down the road in front with Margaret looking for a familiar place.

Margaret excitedly said, "Slow down, stop in front of that bush, that's where the drive-way comes out."

I stopped on the shoulder of the road at the bush and we got out of the car and walked toward the back. Walking along, soon Margaret said, "There it is, that's where the house sits."

"Stand here Margaret and I'll place rocks on the four corners. Motion to me so I get the rocks in exactly the right spots."

I placed four big rocks where the corners of the house should be and Margaret was so thrilled. "That colonial house is going to be

the prettiest house in Turnip Coast. I can almost see it sitting there now."

After that day, every time went go over to our house site to work, the children beg, "Can we go to the four rocks with you?"

Needless to tell you of course, but it took many difficult months, fraught with grief and uncertainty, to get the house, roads, a farm building and a barn built.

But we hired an honest knowledgeable builder with know-how and the proper equipment, which gave excellent results.

A big moving van moved all the fine furniture out of our house in town out to our colonial mansion.

Could we say we went from rags to riches? Well not exactly, but that wouldn't miss the mark by much.

Our money was now getting dangerously low, I knew it was time for me to get busy, catch the spring season and get a big turnip crop planted.

Chapter Thirty-Seven

We deeded the house in town to the city and the city is using it for a Medical Center. Now the ladies of Turnip Coast have a place to go to have their babies.

To all you genial and kind-hearted people, David and Margaret invite you to visit them and their colonial house.

You will find that Turnip Coast is not shown on any map, but there is a way to find that disguised land.

You must search for the most beautiful people on earth. When you find those beautiful people.

You have found Turnip Coast where live David and Margaret Montgomery with their seven beautiful children.

The End